Level
**2**

# The Nature Kid's Guide to
# OCTOPUSES

# DAVID ANDERSON

LP Media Inc. Publishing
Text copyright © 2026 by LP Media Inc.
All rights reserved.



For information address LP Media Inc. Publishing,
30012 Variolite St NW, Princeton MN 55371
www.lpmedia.org

Publication Data

Octopuses
The Nature Kid's Guide to Octopuses — First edition.

Summary: "Learn all about Octopuses, the Nature Kid Way"
— Provided by publisher.

ISBN: 979-8-89818-110-9

[1. Octopuses – Non-Fiction] I. Title.

Title: The Nature Kid's Guide to Octopuses

# CONTENTS

# OCEAN HOMES

DID YOU KNOW?
Octopuses can squeeze through any hole that is bigger than their beak! The beak is the only hard part of their body. Everything else is soft and squishy!

**Swish! An octopus glides towards the reef. It is headed to it's den.**

Octopuses live in salty ocean water. They need this salt to survive, so you will not find them in lakes or rivers.

Octopuses live in both warm and cold ocean waters. The water temperature matters a lot. Each type of Octopus needs a certain temperature range.

Octopuses need places to hide. The open ocean is too dangerous for them.  They look for rocky areas with caves and cracks. Coral reefs make great homes too. Sandy bottoms with shells also work. They squeeze into tiny spaces to stay safe.

# WORLD WIDE

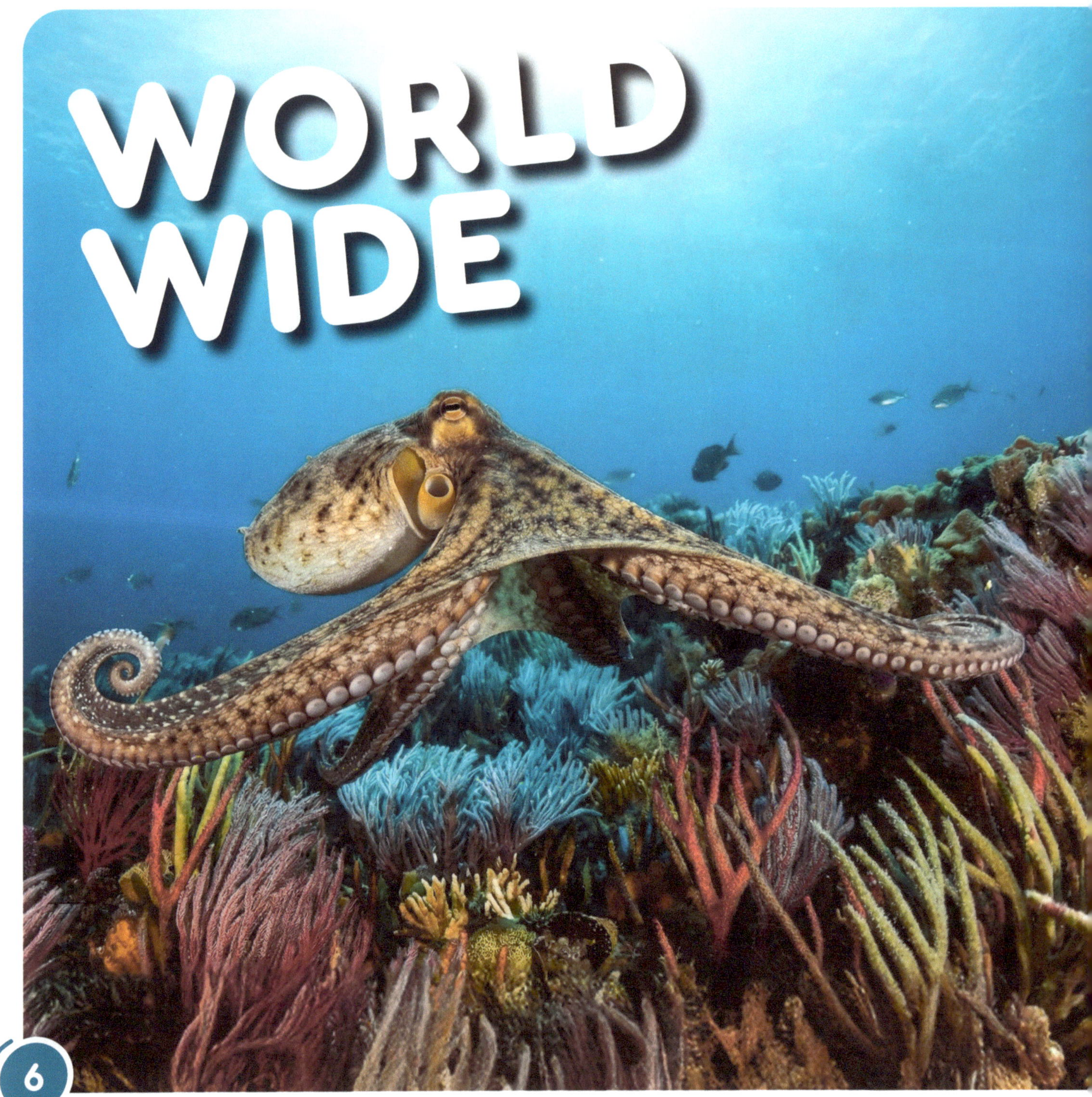

**Swoosh! An octopus glides past a coral reef in Japan.**

Octopuses live in oceans all around the world. They live from the Arctic to the tropics.

The giant Pacific octopus lives near North America and Asia. Common octopuses swim in the Atlantic Ocean.

The blue-ringed octopus lives in shallow waters near Australia. While the dumbo octopus swims deep in the ocean depths. It can go over 13,000 feet down!

The mimic octopus can copy the look of over 15 animals! It changes shape and color to fool predators.

SIZING UP

## Stretch! A small octopus stretches out. It could fit in your hands!

Octopuses come in many sizes. The smallest is the star-sucker pygmy. It can fit on your fingertip!

The giant Pacific octopus is much bigger. It can weigh as much as a large dog. Its arm span can reach 16 feet, which is longer than a car!

The common octopus is medium-sized. It weighs about 6 pounds. That is like a small house cat.

**FUN FACT!**

**The star-sucker pygmy octopus weighs less than a gram. That is lighter than a paperclip!**

# EIGHT ARMS

Two-thirds of an octopus's brain cells are in its arms. Each arm can think alone!

## Click! An octopus spreads it's 8 arms and floats to the reef bottom.

An octopus has eight long arms. Each arm has about 240 **suction cups**. These cups can taste and grip at the same time!

Octopuses have soft bodies with no bones. They can squeeze through tiny holes. A 50-pound octopus can fit through a hole about two inches wide!

Octopuses have three hearts and blue blood. Two hearts pump blood to the **gills**. One heart sends blood to the body. To eat, they use a hard beak in the center of their arms.

# SUPER SENSES

## Squeak! An octopus touches a shell. It can taste it!

Octopuses have excellent eyesight. Their eyes are very sharp, so they can see well in dark water.

Each suction cup can taste and feel. This lets an octopus touch food to know if it is safe to eat. Imagine if you could taste something just by picking it up with your hand!

Octopuses cannot hear like we do. But they can feel vibrations in the water.

**An octopus has about 500 million nerve cells in its body.**

CLEVER
CAMO

## Snap! An octopus changes color. Now it looks like a rock.

Octopuses are masters of disguise. Their skin has special cells that change color in less than one second. They can match rocks, sand, or coral.

They can also change their skin texture. Smooth skin becomes bumpy or spiky. This helps them blend in even better.

Some octopuses copy other animals. The mimic octopus can look like a flatfish or sea snake. This scares **predators** away!

Octopuses are colorblind! Scientists don't know how they know what colors to change to!

# SEAFOOD SNACKS

**Crunch! An octopus catches a crab. It loves tasty seafood!**

Octopuses eat many sea animals. They love crabs, clams, and shrimp. They also eat small fish. They eat snails too.

Octopuses need to eat often. A hungry octopus may eat several crabs in one day. They crack open the shells. They eat the soft parts inside.

Different octopuses like different foods. The giant Pacific octopus eats shrimp and scallops. Smaller octopuses like tiny crabs and mussels.

Some hungry octopuses will eat over 30 crabs each week!

# GRAB IT

FUN
FACT!
Octopuses sometimes drop on
prey from above, like a parachute!
It surprises them.

## Pounce! An octopus grabs a crab. Its arms move fast!

Octopuses are sneaky hunters. They crawl slowly along the ocean floor. They look for **prey** hiding in rocks and sand.

When an octopus spots food, it pounces! It spreads its arms wide like a net. The webbing between its arms traps the prey underneath.

Suction cups grip the prey tightly. These strong suckers make it very hard to escape. Then the octopus uses its hard beak to bite.

Some octopuses dig in the sand for clams. Others reach into tiny cracks to find hiding crabs.

# HUNGRY HUNTERS

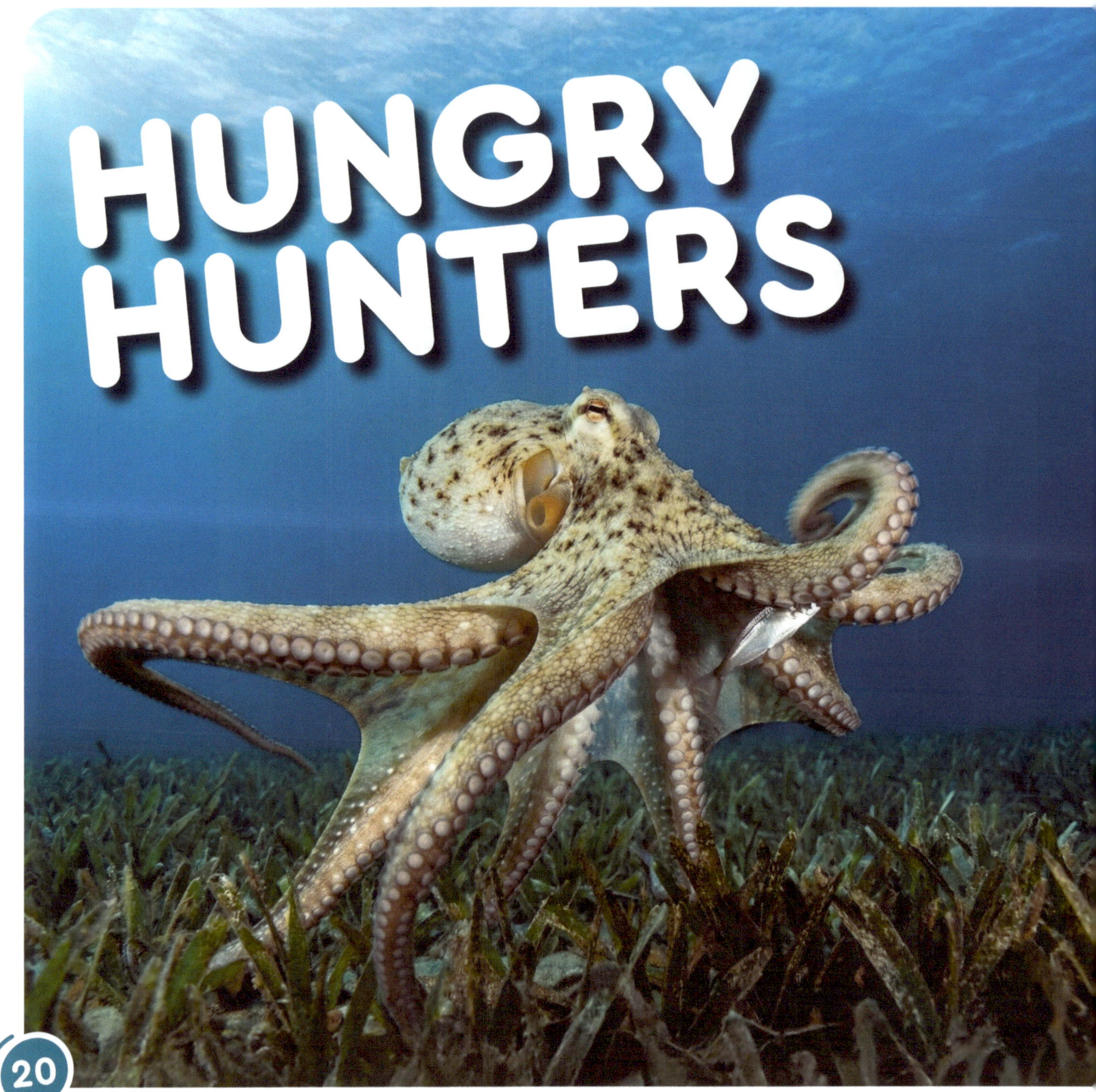

**A hungry Octopus chases a fish away from the reef.  It must get back quickly!**

Many ocean animals hunt octopuses. Sharks are a big threat. Moray eels love to eat them too.

Dolphins are smart hunters. They catch octopuses. They shake them hard to eat them. Seals and sea lions hunt octopuses this way too.

Some fish eat octopuses. Large groupers swallow small ones whole. Whales also snack on octopuses.

Sperm whales can dive thousands of feet deep to hunt octopuses in the darkest parts of the ocean.

# INK AWAY

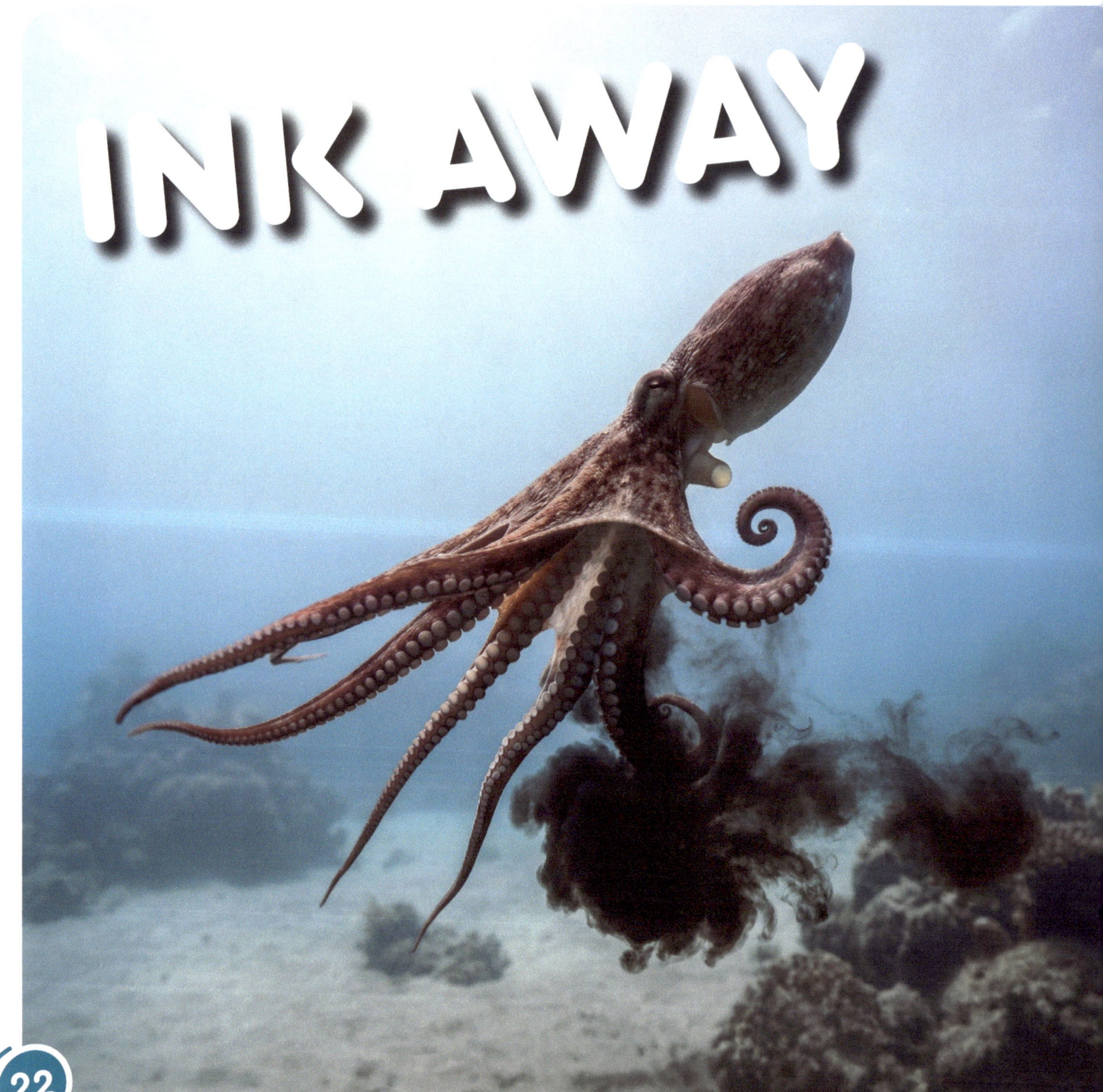

# Poof! A cloud of dark ink fills the water. The octopus jets away!

Octopuses have a special trick to escape danger. They squirt dark ink from their bodies. This ink cloud confuses predators.

The ink hides the octopus from view. It also smells bad to some hunters. This gives the octopus time to swim away fast.

Some octopuses make ink shapes that look like their bodies. Predators attack the fake shape!

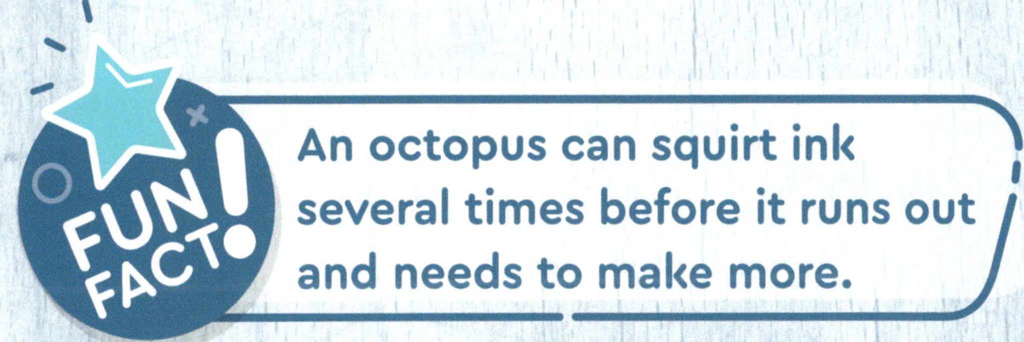

JET SET
24

**Zoom! An octopus shoots through the water. It moves like a rocket!**

Octopuses have three ways to move. They can crawl using their eight arms. Suction cups help them grip rocks and sand.

They also walk on two arms sometimes. The other six arms curl up above them.

For fast escapes, octopuses use jet power. They suck in water and blast it out to zoom away!

**An octopus can jet through water at up to 25 miles per hour. That is faster than most humans run!**

# NIGHT LIFE

## The sun sets over the reef. An octopus wakes up.

Most octopuses are **nocturnal**. This means they are active at night. They sleep during the day in dens.

At night, octopuses come out to hunt. The dark water helps them hide from predators. Their excellent night vision helps them find food.

During the day, octopuses rest in rocky holes. They block the entrance with shells and rocks. This keeps them safe while they sleep.

Octopuses sleep in short bursts. They may take many quick naps instead of one long sleep!

# SOLO STARS

**Rustle! An octopus crawls out of it's den. It is all alone.**

Most octopuses live alone. They do not live in groups or families. Each octopus finds its own den and lives there all by itself.

Octopuses do not have leaders or friends. They only come together to mate. After that, they go right back to living alone.

Some octopuses are not very nice neighbors. If another octopus gets too close, they will chase it away or even throw things at it!

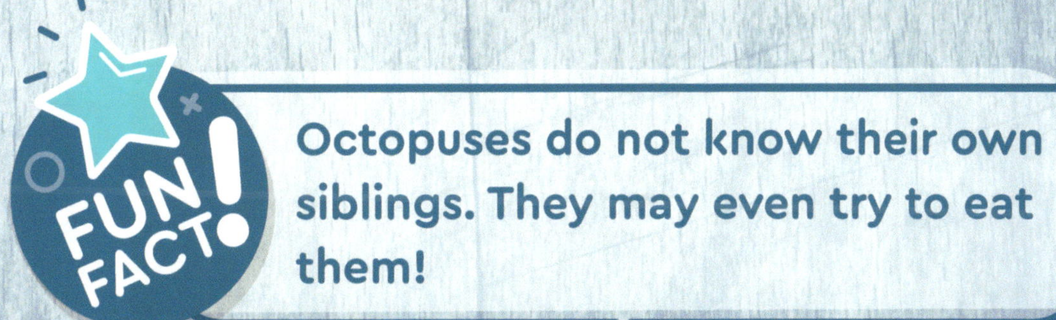

# FINDING MATES

**Grunt! A male octopus waves his arms. He wants to be seen.**

Male octopuses use special displays. They change colors and patterns. Bright stripes and spots appear on their skin.

Males also stretch their arms wide. This makes them look bigger. Some males even flash colors very fast.

Most octopuses only mate once in their lives. After mating, their life cycle ends. This is natural for these amazing animals.

One species called the argonaut octopus detaches its mating arm and sends it swimming over to the female all by itself!

# TINY TOTS

Baby octopuses are born knowing how to hunt. They catch tiny shrimp on their very first day of life!

**Swish! Tiny baby octopuses float in the sea. They are so tiny!**

Newborn octopuses hatch from eggs. A mother can lay up to 200,000 eggs at once!

These babies are incredibly tiny. Some are smaller than a grain of rice. They look like miniature adults with eight little arms.

The babies float near the surface at first. They drift with the ocean currents. As they grow, they sink down to the seafloor and start to crawl and hunt like adult octopuses.

Being tiny is dangerous. Fish, crabs, and even jellyfish eat baby octopuses. Out of every thousand babies that hatch, only one or two will grow up to be adults.

# MIGHTY MOMS

DID YOU KNOW?
After her babies hatch, the mother octopus dies within days.

## A mother octopus guards her eggs. She will not leave them.

Mother octopuses are very dedicated. A female stays with her eggs the whole time they grow. She does not eat while she guards them.

She gently blows water over the eggs. This keeps them clean and gives them oxygen. She also pushes away dirt and animals that come too close.

Mothers can guard eggs for weeks or even months. The giant Pacific octopus watches her eggs for up to seven months! After all this care, baby octopuses must survive on their own. Their mother will not be around to protect them.

# BIG BRAINS

**An octopus senses a crab in a tiny space.  It must figure out how to get it out.**

Octopuses are very smart. They have no backbone. But they have big brains. They have about 500 million nerve cells. These cells help them learn. They help them remember too.

Octopuses can solve problems. They can use tools. The veined octopus carries coconut shells. It uses them as a shelter.

Being smart helps octopuses survive.

**Octopuses can open jars from the inside! They unscrew the lids. Scientists use puzzle jars to test their intelligence.**

# SPOT ONE

## A diver spots an octopus swimming from it's den. What a find!

The best place to see an octopus is at the aquarium. There you can watch octopuses up close and safely.

If you visit the ocean, look in tide pools. You might spot a small octopus hiding under rocks. Never touch or poke it. Just watch quietly.

Look for color changes and arm movements. To see these, stay calm and keep your distance.

Some aquariums train octopuses to know their keepers. They may squirt water at strangers!

# GLOSSARY

### suction cups
Round pads on an octopus's arms that can stick to things and taste at the same time.

### nocturnal
An animal that sleeps during the day and is awake at night.

### gills
Body parts that let ocean animals breathe underwater.

### predators
Animals that hunt and eat other animals.

### prey
An animal that is hunted and eaten by another animal.